BLUFF AND BRAN
and the Snowdrift

by Meg Rutherford
Illustrated by the Author

PICTURE CORGI BOOKS

Also by Meg Rutherford,
and published by Picture Corgi Books:
BLUFF AND BRAN AND THE TREEHOUSE

PRINTING HISTORY

BLUFF AND BRAN AND THE SNOWDRIFT

A PICTURE CORGI BOOK 0 552 525669

Originally published in Great Britain by Andrè Deutsch Limited

PRINTING HISTORY
Andrè Deutsch edition published 1987
Picture Corgi edition published 1989

Picture Corgi books are published by Transworld Publishers Ltd.,
61-63 Uxbridge Road, Ealing, London W5 5SA, in Australia by
Transworld Publishers (Australia) Pty. Ltd., 15-23 Helles Avenue,
Moorebank, NSW 2170, and in New Zealand by Transworld
Publishers (N.Z.) Ltd., Cnr. Moselle and Waipareira Avenues,
Henderson, Auckland.

Made and printed in Portugal by Printer Portugesa

It was Christmas, and the little girl was taking Bluff and Bran to visit her cousin in the country. Bluff didn't like her new travelling basket.

She refused to get into it . . .

and hid.

The little girl gave up trying. She put Bran into the basket instead, then left the room. Bluff looked at the basket, then at Bran, then she squeezed in beside him. It really was quite comfortable.

The family set off.
Bluff wore a collar with the cousin's address on it
. . . just in case she got lost.

It was late at night when they arrived at the cousin's house.

In the morning, Bran was given a smart new suit to keep him warm, then he and Bluff went outside with the little girls.

They couldn't see any other houses or people. Just miles and miles of bumpy hills and some trees. The stream below the wall had frozen over. Bluff went off to explore.

She found a Christmas Tree in a tub, and jumped up to hide under its branches. It smelled of forests, rich and fragrant. The family came out and took the tree indoors to decorate it.

As they carried it, Bluff played with
the swaying tips of its long soft branches.
She quite forgot Bran.

Indoors, boxes and baubles and ribbons and crispy crinkly coloured paper were piled around the tree.
Bluff had never had such fun.

She leaped and rolled, and pushed the baubles round the floor.
She teased the ribbons, tore the paper,
and jumped in and out of boxes.

Outside, it began to snow,
and soon Bran
was completely covered.

Suddenly Bluff remembered him. She ran outside so quickly that no one saw her leave. She could hardly see through the snowflakes, and there was no sign of Bran.

None of the snowy shapes looked like him. She dug into every one, but none of them was Bran. Then, just as the snow stopped falling, she found a paw . . .

and pounced in pleasure.

WHOOF! The snowy mound exploded . . .

. . . and FLOFF!
went Bluff and Bran as they slithered faster and
faster down the snowy slope towards the frozen stream below.

Bluff lurched after Bran as he rolled,
and as he rolled he turned into
a snowball!

Down they went,
faster and faster, right into the middle of . . .

. . . a snowdrift. And silence. Then there was a splintering sound

...nd they floated away from the bank, and down the stream . . .

. . .and past some cows.

Bluff wasn't sure about the cows. They looked big and rather spikey, and there were lots of them. Nearby was a narrow bridge where the snow and ice packed tight,

so Bluff pulled Bran off the ice-floe,
and up the bank away from the cows.

But the cows crossed the bridge, and came to stare at Bluff and Bran.
One came quite close, and breathed all over them, frightening Bluff.
With all her courage she went up to it,

HISSED . . . and

then ran up the nearest tree. Poor Bran. He was all alone again.
The cows closed in.

Then the farmer came to fetch his cows. He noticed the address on Bluff's collar, and gently picked her up and carried her back with Bran to the cousin's house.

The little girl was crying. She hugged Bluff and Bran and made them snug in front of the fire. Then she thanked the farmer. 'We've been out looking for them for hours,' she sobbed, 'we thought that they were drowned.'

The little girl and her cousin lit the lights on the Christmas Tree. They were happy now, and so were Bluff and Bran, who were dry at last. Tomorrow would be Christmas Day, when everyone would have their presents. But Bluff and Bran had theirs after supper.

It was their very own Christmas Cottage, and they thought it was wonderful.